# Shivaree

## A Play In Two Acts

## by William Mastrosimone

A SAMUEL FRENCH ACTING EDITION

**SAMUEL FRENCH**

FOUNDED 1830

New York Hollywood London Toronto

SAMUELFRENCH.COM

*This Play is dedicated to*

*Cabby #407*

*and the man in the window
with the disease of kings*

*Mirko Tuma*

*and Niema*

*Special thanks to Dan Sullivan*

Shivaree was presented by The Seattle Repertory Theatre on November 9, 1983. The cast was as follows:

CHANDLER ......................... Steven Flynn
SCAGG.............................John Procaccino
MARY ANN .......................... Diane Kagan
LAURA...............................Lori Larsen
SHIVAREE .......................... Maggie Baird

Directed by........................Daniel Sullivan
Stage Manager ......................Diane DiVita
Set Designer ....................Robert Dahlstrom
Costume Designer .................Sally Richardson
Lighting Designer ...............Michael Davidson
Sound by ......................... Michael Holten

The production transferred to The Long Wharf Theatre in New Haven, Connecticut on February 7, 1984.

Artistic Director .................... Arvin Brown
Lighting Designed by...............Ronald Wallace
Production Stage Manager........... George Darveris

# SHIVAREE

TIME: Now
PLACE: The South

## SET

An apartment with:

A small window equipped with an air conditioner

French doors that open to a balcony about five feet from another balcony of the next house.

A skylight

A telescope mounted on a tripod

An interior door that leads downstairs

A bed

Aquaria with exotic fish, turtles, all with pumps, special lights

A formicary (optional)

Aquarium with hamster with a treadmill (optional)

Tons of books (perhaps the walls are made of books)

Plants and flowers everywhere

A pully connected to a beam which hangs a cluster of bananas

A C.B. radio

A conspicuous I.V. rack with clear plastic tubes hanging

An expensive computer and large screen

Everything is padded or rounded off; nothing sharp; all is white, like a clinic, to detect blood.

## CAST

CHANDLER KIMBROUGH
MARY ANN KIMBROUGH
SCAGG
LAURA
SHIVAREE

MUSIC: Something from the Italian Renaissance

# Shivaree

## ACT ONE

*Let the stars appear one by one. Give the sky a gradual moon whose light reflects prettily on the white lace curtains of the French doors and open window. Rose-colored heat lightning is the only illumination. No thunder. Wind chimes, of bamboo, lack breeze. Outside the window an occasional bat flits by in pursuit of the greenish glow of fireflies. Faraway, the caterwaul of cats in heat make eerie music. CHANDLER turns the music off, opens a bag, takes out an ascot, peels off sales tag, puts it on, puts on Johnny Mathis, "Misty,"\* stands before his mirror.*

CHANDLER. How do you do? Won't you sit down? (*new pose*) How do you do? Won't you sit down? (*turns off the music, opens artbook of Botticelli's paintings; to himself—simply because the sound pleases him:*) Simonetta. (*He gets a "Playboy" out of hiding, compares, and recites as if cramming for an exam.*) Mons veneris. Labia majora. Labia minora. Mucus membrane secretes a viscous fluid when stimulated which acts as a lubricant and thus facilitates copulation. (*He takes a skin-magazine out of hiding, opens it up to the centerfold. He opens an artbook of Botticelli's paintings and compares. Caterwaul.*) One hundred and forty million. One hundred and forty million. A million

---

\*Note: permission to produce SHIVAREE does not include permission to use this song in production. Permission ought to be procured from the copyright owner of the song.

is a thousand thousands. And that times 140 is one hundred and forty million sperms per ejaculation. I am one out of one hundred and forty million. It's like the Boston Marathon! And I won! (*The buzzer rings. He rushes to it.*) Who's there?

SCAGG. (*over intercom*) Fudgie wudgie, creamsicle, Eskimo pie, fur pie!

CHANDLER. Are you alone?

SCAGG. Open up, amigo.

(*CHANDLER releases the door lock, puts on his suit jacket, preens up. Enter SCAGG in white pants, white shirt, white shoes and panama hat with a feather lugging a white metal box on shoulder straps with cartoon characters painted on the side.*)

SCAGG. (*continued*) M'man! m'man! M'main man!

CHANDLER. Where is she?

SCAGG. The whore's in the truck and I'm double parked. —Lay alittle cash on me, bro.

CHANDLER. Let me open the wine so it can breathe. (*SCAGG opens the metal box, takes out a brown liquor store bag.*)

SCAGG. Let there be juice!

CHANDLER. What is this?

SCAGG. The *wine*.

CHANDLER. This isn't Medoc.

SCAGG. *Medoc?* I thought you said Mad Dog.

CHANDLER. I never heard of this! Where's the corkscrew!

SCAGG. This is 20th century technology—you don't need one for this wine, Amigo.

CHANDLER. O God, Scagg! This is awful!

SCAGG. What's the button here? Quick k.o.? For a five-spot more you got genuine mountain corn brew. Goes down hot, lays 'em out cold. (*taking a mason jar of clear moonshine from the metal box*) — On special.

CHANDLER. I don't want that!

SCAGG. Fudgie-wudgie?

CHANDLER. No! Did you forget the candles?

SCAGG. Only the best for m'man! (*taking votive candles from the box*)

CHANDLER. These are *used!* Where'd you get these?

SCAGG. The church on the corner.

CHANDLER. You robbed these from the church!

SCAGG. Hell, m'man, they had a whole shitload.

CHANDLER. O, God, Scagg.

SCAGG. M'man, these are consecrated.

CHANDLER. Did you tell her about, you know, me?

SCAGG. Yup.

CHANDLER. How'd you tell her?

SCAGG. Just like you told me.

CHANDLER. How?

SCAGG. I said I got a friend, he's a hypodermiac . . .

CHANDLER. Hemophiliac.

SCAGG. Right. Right.

CHANDLER. And what was her reaction?

SCAGG. Gooseegg.

CHANDLER. Really?

CHANDLER. What color's her hair?

SCAGG. Just like you wanted.

CHANDLER. She pretty?

SCAGG. Pretty?

CHANDLER. Really?

SCAGG. Any man with red blood in his vein would crawl five hundred miles on hands and knees over broken beer bottles and armadilla turds just to'hear this enchalada burp.

CHANDLER. O, God, Scagg, she's not cheap, is she?

SCAGG. Fifty bucks.

CHANDLER. No! Is she slutty-looking?

SCAGG. In her spare time she poses for madonna pictures.

CHANDLER. How long's her hair?

SCAGG. About here.

CHANDLER. That's — short!

SCAGG. Whattaya gonna do with a hank o'hair?

CHANDLER. I asked you to regard that!

SCAGG. You want hair, I'll get ya a sheepdog cheaper.

CHANDLER. I specifically stipulated length *and* color.

SCAGG. M'man, it ain't like shopping at the A&P.

CHANDLER. Does she look like this? (*showing the Botticelli book*)

SCAGG. That what you want? A born-again Billy Gramm girl?

CHANDLER. She's not like this? What's so funny?

SCAGG. One leg's longer than the other.

CHANDLER. She's not like this?

SCAGG. Alittle. Only thing, she's got a very mild case of herpes.

CHANDLER. O God!

SCAGG. C'mon, bro! I'm only goosin ya!

CHANDLER. Everything's gone awry! (*SCAGG rolls back his long sleeve, revealing a dozen watches.*)

SCAGG. I got a good deal on a watch.

CHANDLER. I don't want a watch! What will the cost be for, you know, just the woman?

SCAGG. Fifty.

CHANDLER. I don't mean to impugn your integrity, but is that normal?

SCAGG. Plus ten for the vino.

CHANDLER. For that?

SCAGG. Candles on me. And five for this. (*taking out a packet from the box*) This'll drive her t'loonsville, jack.

SCAGG. French tickler.

CHANDLER. I don't want that!

SCAGG. Take the watch, I throw in the tickler.

CHANDLER. No.

SCAGG. Want another magazine?

CHANDLER. No.

SCAGG. Then we're up to fifty plus ten, — that's sixty five dollars.

CHANDLER. Sixty.

SCAGG. Right, plus ten for my time. Seventy. Grass?

CHANDLER. No.

SCAGG. Coke?

CHANDLER. No.

SCAGG. Just askin. (*CHANDLER goes to a hiding place, takes out a pillow case filled with coins of every denomination neatly wrapped. SCAGG takes out a tiny tin.*) Tigar Balm?

CHANDLER. What's that?

SCAGG. Tiger balm. Extract from the horn of the white rhino. Gives ya a stone bone.

CHANDLER. I don't need an aphrodisiac.

SCAGG. 'Course ya don't. Not now. Don't need an umbrella when the sun's shinin, do ya?

CHANDLER. How much?

SCAGG. Now, m'man, there's three, four, maybe five rhinoes rottin on the plains o'Sergengeti t'fill this little tin — but it's enough for half a lifetime.

CHANDLER. How much?

SCAGG. Top shelf, m'man. Seventy-five.

CHANDLER. Can I owe it to you?

SCAGG. Nothin' walks 'less the president talks.

CHANDLER. I can't afford it.

SCAGG. My cost—twenty five.

CHANDLER. Can't afford it.

MARY. (*on c.b.*) Mobile to Home Base, c'mon.

CHANDLER. Stand still! Don't breathe! She's got ears! Home Base to Mobile, over.

MARY. Whattcha doin, babe? Over.

CHANDLER. Reading. Over.

MARY. Want some ice cream? Over.

CHANDLER. Negatory, Mom, but thanks. What's your 10-20?

MARY. Just dropped off a fare downtown, honey babe. Conventioneers are comin' on like locusts. Catch ya on the flip-flop, honey babe.

CHANDLER. Forty Rodger.

SCAGG. Gimmie the money—I'll bring her up.

CHANDLER. Could we postpone this?

SCAGG. Goddamn, I went out of my way to get you a woman—not just a woman, but one with hair, and this, and that. Damn, boy, you know how much business I lost?

CHANDLER. I'm sorry.

SCAGG. Sorry ain't gonna help me pay your mama the rent tomorrow.

CHANDLER. She suspects something.

SCAGG. Use my room.

CHANDLER. But if I'm not here when she calls, she'll come looking.

SCAGG. She won't look for you *there*. You leave by the roomer's entrance, come back in your private entrance. Say you went for a walk.

CHANDLER. Oh . . . I don't know . . .

SCAGG. Now you decide right now if you wanna ride or slide.

CHANDLER. I planned this for a year!

SCAGG. Ride or slide.

CHANDLER. Ride.

SCAGG. Lay some cash on me bro. – What's that?

CHANDLER. The money.

SCAGG. Don't you have paper?

CHANDLER. I've hoarded loose change for over a year. It's the only way I get money. For the ice cream.

SCAGG. How am I gonna pay her with 97 pounds o'coin?

CHANDLER. Ten, twenty, thirty, forty.

SCAGG. This is a real ass-pain.

CHANDLER. Fifty, sixty, sixty-five, seventy.

SCAGG. This is a real snafu, m'man.

CHANDLER. Should we postpone it?

SCAGG. I don't know if she's gonna take it.

CHANDLER. Wait!

SCAGG. What?

CHANDLER. I have to ask you something.

SCAGG. You want the tickler.

CHANDLER. No! When you bring her up . . .

SCAGG. Yeah.

CHANDLER. And you leave us, right?

SCAGG. Not 'less you want me t'cheerlead . . . Chandler, Chandler, he's m'man, if he can't do it . . .

CHANDLER. Scagg! C'mon! This is important!

SCAGG. Sorry, Amigo.

CHANDLER. When it's just me and her, what do I do? – I mean, I know what to do, but – how would you, say, get things started?

SCAGG. Hang loose, drink a little juice, and the one-eyed worm'll find its way home.

CHANDLER. Scagg, concerning the actual womanly part?

SCAGG. Yeah.

CHANDLER. Could we possibly discuss that a little?

SCAGG. I can talk all night about the vertical smile. I seen dogs rip open jugglers for it; bulls break down barn doors for it; roosters chew chicken wire t'get in the coop. I seen cowboys get throwed off a brama — o'purpose! — just t'snag the fancy o'some freckled little pony tail up in the bleechers! You can't name the things a male won't do for that little patch o'real estate no bigger than a fried egg.

CHANDLER. What was that?

SCAGG. What?

CHANDLER. My mother's cab. She just pulled up.

SCAGG. Holy shit!

CHANDLER. Go down the back way. We'll do it another night.

SCAGG. No, I'll bring the woman when your mama goes.

(*CHANDLER hides the wine, shuts out the light, jumps into bed, pulls the covers to his chin, but his shoes are visible. Enter MARY KIMBROUGH dressed as a cabby.*)

MARY. Lovy? You asleep?

CHANDLER. Mom?

MARY. Y'up?

CHANDLER. Hmmm?

MARY. Whatcha doin?

CHANDLER. Sleeping.

MARY. How's m'baby? All dressed for bed? Your best suit, eh? Where ya goin in your dreams?

CHANDLER. I wanted to see if the suit still fits and must've dozed off. I thought you were downtown.

MARY. I had a nearby fare. You must be roasted out of your mind. Lookie, honey babe, you got the air conditioner off! And the window open!

CHANDLER. I hate the noise, that hum.

MARY. That damn screw's loose again. (*takes out a screwdriver*)

CHANDLER. I'd rather have fresh air.

MARY. Air's not fresh. It's all chemicals.

CHANDLER. There's a river breeze.

MARY. Putrid air. Factory air. Poison air. Nosir. (*She closes the window and turns on the air conditioner; pause.*) You seen that ice cream man?

CHANDLER. No.

MARY. You take plasma?

CHANDLER. Yes.

MARY. What for?

CHANDLER. I scraped my gums with the toothbrush.

MARY. Where?

CHANDLER. It's alright.

MARY. Let's see.

CHANDLER. It's alright.

MARY. Don't brush so hard.

CHANDLER. Alright.

MARY. Don't frown on me. Remember your last tooth-pull.

CHANDLER. Every quart.

MARY. So whattcha been doin'?

CHANDLER. After supper I watched a somniferous documentary on TV on Grey Whales. I weeded the garden. We have a big slug problem, you know. One third of the tomatoes are destroyed. I called the library. Mrs. Yarborough gave me a list of books on slug defense.

MARY. Beer.

CHANDLER. Pardon?

MARY. Stale beer attracts 'em. Put it around in little bowls. They smell it, think its the mating scent, crawl up the bowl, fall in and drown in their own sin.

CHANDLER. O, mom, you made that up.

MARY. Old time remedy, goes way back. Look it up in your books. I know a thing or two, sonny boy. We come from farm people, ya know.

CHANDLER. Drown in sin.

MARY. You shush. I heard ya talking on the c.b. with a trucker.

CHANDLER. Coalminer. "Eh, good buddy, t'day m' dog had pups and et one."

MARY. Well, you can't expect everybody t'be on your level honeybabe. So you ain't seen that ice cream man anytime today?

CHANDLER. I got an eskimo pie from him when I was in the garden.

MARY. I told you I don't want you buyin ice cream from him. If you want something, just call me.

CHANDLER. I didn't want to bother you.

MARY. It's no bother. Did he come up here?

CHANDLER. No. O, I forgot—Teddy called.

MARY. What's he want? Zif I didn't know.

CHANDLER. He's free to put in the other skylight, which means he wouldn't mind spending a few days here, which means he still wants to marry you.

MARY. Son of a bee! You never mind.

CHANDLER. You promised me a skylight, Mom.

MARY. Skylight—not a daddy. Now you pick out a nice shirt in the Sears and Roebuck Catalogue so you look nice and handsome for the races tomorrow.

CHANDLER. Can you afford to take off?

MARY. Half a day. We'll fix a little chicken and lemonade, park by the gate, see the whole thing.

CHANDLER. O, we can't go inside?

MARY. Now, now sugar. All those uppity ladies swingin brand new handbags, and roughhousers carousin and carryin' on, nosir. We'll park by the gate. You bring your binoculars.

CHANDLER. And then the planetarium.

MARY. OK.

CHANDLER. And then the museum.

MARY. Now, now honeybabe. Little school kids yellin and runnin up and down the stairs? No-sir. How I ever let you talk me into this thing (*pulling his ascot out of his shirt*) you look like one o'them Hollywood outlaws. You thumb through and pick out a nice shirt and I'll pick it up in the morning.

CHANDLER. I don't need a new shirt, Mom.

MARY. Sure you do.

CHANDLER. The closet's full.

MARY. This one's frayed on the sleeve, this one's crooked. I swear the way they make clothes today, no pride, no pride in workmanship. These are gone in the rag bag. Now c'mon, lovy, pick one out. Lookie here. Do you like this shirt? (*She tears shirts into rags.*)

CHANDLER. Do they have it in a round collar?

MARY. That's too old fashioned. You like this one?

CHANDLER. Either.

MARY. Blue or white?

CHANDLER. (*pause*) Yellow or pink.

MARY. No, no, honey, that's not for you. You want to look distinguished.

CHANDLER. Blue.

MARY. Well, you got alot of blues.

CHANDLER. White?

MARY. That's a good choice. (*pause*) And I'll see if they have a round collar.

CHANDLER. And would you pick up these books at the library?

MARY. Mrs. Yarborough says you got an overdue book. Dollar ninety-five.

CHANDLER. Could we afford to buy a copy of this book?

MARY. You got so many books, lovy. I think next year I'll have that wall knocked out, put up a greenhouse for ya, and that observatory ya want, and your own bathroom so ya don't have to go trudging up and down the stairs.

CHANDLER. Teddy could do a masterful job with that.

MARY. Now you never you mind about Teddy! And hang that suit up!

CHANDLER. And would you stop by Mrs. Vollens? She has some knickknacks for me.

MARY. Like what?

CHANDLER. Jerry's parachute.

MARY. You ain't jumpin outta no airplanes!

CHANDLER. I only want to make a canopy over the bed.

MARY. Son of a bee—she call you?

CHANDLER. No.

MARY. You call her?

CHANDLER. Yes.

MARY. I don't want you talkin' with sucha women.

CHANDLER. Alright.

MARY. She oughta be on death row. No mom in the hemophillia chapter even talks to her. Lettin her boy go jumpin outta airplanes!

CHANDLER. Jerry made twenty-seven jumps. He had special shoes and padding, and jumped on sand.

MARY. Did it help him when he landed on that barbed wire fence?

CHANDLER. It was a freak accident.

MARY. She was a freak mother, and why you want a deadman's thing, I'll never know.

CHANDLER. I loved how he talked about his life being cleaved in two, prejump and postjump.

MARY. That's just how her heart's cleaved. I held her hand there in the 'mergency room when they was pumping 23 quarts o' blood in her boy. Nosir. Can't allow it. Nosir. So you get your mind off daring-do. You are what you are. (*pause*) Where's the overdue book?

CHANDLER. I'd like to have it renewed.

MARY. This is the third time, lovy.

CHANDLER. Then never mind.

MARY. I will, I will, it's just not like you t'keep a book more than two days. What is this?

CHANDLER. Botticelli. Paintings.

MARY. Nudies, eh?

CHANDLER. Art. That's "Primavera." That's "The Birth of Venus."

MARY. Looks like a naked woman on the half-shell t'me. (*The skin magazine falls out.*)

CHANDLER. That damn Scagg.

MARY. That his?

CHANDLER. He had it.

MARY. Had it?

CHANDLER. It's his.

MARY. Did he give it to you?

CHANDLER. No. He had it with him and he must've left it here by mistake.

MARY. Well you make sure he gets it back.

CHANDLER. Yes ma'm.

MARY. I'll give it him.

CHANDLER. Yes, ma'm.

MARY. That goddamn Scagg! He's a pedigree bum, a drinker, therefore a liar, therefore thief, therefore trouble. What's he get from you?

CHANDLER. Nothing.

MARY. Nosir, don't buy it. Life's always tit for tat. (*pause*) I don't want him up here no more. Or anybody else I rent to.

CHANDLER. Yes, ma'am.

MARY. You're special. (*She hugs him, checks his ears for wax.*) He's out o' here tomorrow, I swear I could rip him apart with my hands! — just the looks of 'im sticks in my craw.

CHANDLER. Then why'd you rent him a room?

MARY. Damn if I wouldn't rent to Beezlebub if he could fork up thirty advance rent and thirty security for damages. I'm just glad your daddy ain't here d'see how I carved up his dream home t'rent rooms by the week. If he saw me now heavin suitcases bigger than me in the taxi? — Your daddy was such a man. Wouldn't let me so much as lift a sugar-spoon. When he carried me over the threshhold, down in the vestibule, I said, what we gonna do with all these rooms? He said fill 'em with kids. And that's just what I did. All the world's socks without a mate, all the shoes without a double, end up here. All the bastard kids of the world. — Kiss good night, lovy. Brush your teeth, k?

CHANDLER. I did.

MARY. Brush 'em again for me.

CHANDLER. Going to bed now?

MARY. No. There's some good business at the airport now.

CHANDLER. Don't take any creeps, ok?

MARY. Don't you worry 'bout your momma. I got a left hand to shame Sugar Ray Leonard. Night night, lovy.

CHANDLER. Night, mom. — Bring home some stale beer — we're going to drown 'em in sin!

MARY. Hang up your suit and don't wait up for me. (*Exit MARY with the books. CHANDLER waits for her foot-falls to die away, and begins to undress. He unbuttons his vest, undoes his ascot, etc.*)

CHANDLER. Did you hear about Chandler? (*pause*) They found him dead. (*pause*) They found him on the walk. They're calling it suicide. (*pause*) They're calling it accidental. Someone saw him hanging out the window waving down the ice cream man. They think he slipped. (*pause*) What a karma: to die for an Eskimo Pie. (*pause*) They're calling it natural causes. (*pause*) They found a brain tumor the size of an orange. Not mandarine. Florida. Lodged in the medulla oblongata. Very rare—only kills one out of every one hundred and forty million. (*Buzzer sounds.*) Who's there?

SCAGG. A man and a lady. Open up, amigo. (*CHANDLER pushes the lock-release button. CHANDLER tidies up. We hear footfalls up the stairs. Enter SCAGG.*) Everything's ace high m'man unless your zipper snags.

CHANDLER. I said we'd do it another night!

(*Enter LAURA.*)

SCAGG. This is Laura.

CHANDLER. How do you do?

LAURA. You must be Chandelier.

CHANDLER. Chandler.

LAURA. Chandler.

SCAGG. See here, m'man—just like in the book—left leg's longer than the other.

CHANDLER. Shut up!

SCAGG. Adios.

CHANDLER. No, have a drink, Scagg.

SCAGG. Ain't you never heard three's a crowd.

LAURA. In my neighborhood they say three's almost as much fun as four.

SCAGG. Chandler, Chandler, he's m'man—

CHANDLER. Go on! (*Exit SCAGG, laughing.*) How do you do?

LAURA. Hi.

CHANDLER. Won't you sit down?

LAURA. I am.

CHANDLER. At the table?

LAURA. Oh, you like it on the table?

CHANDLER. No. No. I mean . . .

LAURA. Look, I understand. I do a guy who's into closets.

CHANDLER. No, I mean for a drink of wine or tea or . . . that's all I have. Scagg brought this wine. Not having drunk it, I can't testify as to its merits.

LAURA. What's the matter?

CHANDLER. I don't remember where I hid it. I didn't want my . . . well, actually I wanted to put it where it wouldn't get broken.

LAURA. Scagg said it's goodnight if you get cut.

CHANDLER. That's not true.

LAURA. I had a client do a massive coronary on me once. Thing was, I didn't know and kept going.

CHANDLER. I wish I could remember . . . I was here and . . .

LAURA. That's ok. I don't need any wine.

CHANDLER. Do you like music?

LAURA. I'd gut my dog if I thought it'd make a good sound.

CHANDLER. What would you like to hear?

LAURA. Whatever brings ya to a head, sweetheart. (*CHANDLER puts on a tape.*) You read all these books?

CHANDLER. Yes.

LAURA. I like brains.

CHANDLER. Pardon?

LAURA. Brains. I like em.

CHANDLER. I'm a bibliophile.

LAURA. O, I'm sorry. (*The music comes on. It's Johnny Mathis singing "Misty."* LAURA *bursts out laughing.*)

CHANDLER. Would you prefer something else?

LAURA. No, love, it's fabulous. Relax.

CHANDLER. I am.

LAURA. No you're not. Really. Let yourself go.

CHANDLER. Thank you.

LAURA. Let's sit on the bed and talk about it.

CHANDLER. Momentarily.

LAURA. It's alright, love, 'least you don't want t'pour teryaki sauce all over me.

CHANDLER. Pardon?

LAURA. Nothin'. You still looking for that wine?

CHANDLER. Yes.

LAURA. Wouldn't you rather undress me?

CHANDLER. I would really like to have some wine first.

LAURA. You wanna do this some other time?

CHANDLER. Would that be inconvenient?

LAURA. I'm booked all week what with the A.M.A. and Shriners conventions.

CHANDLER. No. Now. Tonight.

LAURA. So we gotta rise to the occasion 'cause I got other people to see.

CHANDLER. O.

LAURA. You thought I'd stay all night?

CHANDLER. Well, yes.

LAURA. It's a hundred big ones for all night, babe.

---

*See note, page 7.

CHANDLER. I didn't know.

LAURA. Otherwise, it's thirty-five a throw.

CHANDLER. Thirty-five?

LAURA. For a straight jump.

CHANDLER. What else's, you know, available?

LAURA. Well, there's straight, half and half, doggie-doggie, 'round the world.

CHANDLER. Fine.

LAURA. You want the works?

CHANDLER. Sure.

LAURA. Whoa, wild man, — that's two hundred and fifty plus mucho stamina.

CHANDLER. O. O, I see. Let's . . . just regular.

LAURA. Well, let's get the fish in the pan here, babe.

CHANDLER. I'm not quite ready.

LAURA. Want me to talk filthy?

CHANDLER. No. Thank you.

LAURA. Wis un accent, eh, amor?

CHANDLER. Thank you just the same.

LAURA. Wanna just shoot the breeze awhile?

CHANDLER. Would that be possible?

LAURA. Walter used to have to talk first.

CHANDLER. Walter?

LAURA. Philosophy Proff, Tuesday nights.

CHANDLER. Really? What'd he talk about?

LAURA. Talked about them Greek boys and diabolical materialism. Hooked up a garden hose to the exhaust pipe, sat in the back seat, and there went my education. — So what should we talk about?

CHANDLER. Why did he kill himself?

LAURA. The man had a thing about, you know, reality . . . all that about — I can think therefore I'm here.

CHANDLER. "I think therefore I am."

LAURA. They changed it?

CHANDLER. No. It's still the same.

LAURA. So, let's talk about the planets. — What's that?

CHANDLER. That's an artist's conception of the origin of our universe. It's called the BIG BANG THEORY.

LAURA. I know that theory. Feel better? Good. Let's go.

CHANDLER. Please! — Please don't squeeze my wrist so hard.

LAURA. What'd I do.

CHANDLER. I bruise quite easily.

LAURA. Jesus. What is this thing you've got?

CHANDLER. Blood disorder. Not contagious. Inherited. Actually it's the lack of a protein the blood plasma which regulates the time it takes for blood to clot.

LAURA. That's a real bitch. Can I undress you?

CHANDLER. (*pause*) Yes. (*She begins to undress him.*)

LAURA. What a fine ascot. Silk? Relax. Your neck's so tight. Let your arms just hang down. Sure. Yes. Yes. Relax. Touch me. Not there. Somewheres else. Close your eyes. Close 'em. Shh! Don't talk. Touch my belly. Yes. That's where it all is. You are such a lovely man.

(*MARY's voice interrupts over c.b.*)

MARY. (*on c.b.*) Mobile to Home Base, copy?

LAURA. Police!

CHANDLER. Don't move! Please! Don't make a sound!

LAURA. I'm on probation. You got a back door here? (*grabbing her belongings in a rush*)

CHANDLER. Please! It's my mom!

MARY. Mobile to Home Base, c'mon!

CHANDLER. Home Base to Mobile, copy?

MARY. Wall to wall, treetop tall. Sorry to wake you sugar, but I'm taking some oil people over to the Palm Room and I won't be home till very late, so don't you worry none, k?

CHANDLER. OK.

MARY. Sugar? You brush your teeth?

CHANDLER. Yes, ma'm.

MARY. Dental Floss?

CHANDLER. Yes, ma'm.

MARY. Brush 'em again, honeybabe.

CHANDLER. Yes, ma'm.

MARY. Night, night, lovy. Over.

CHANDLER. Good night. Over.

LAURA. Your mama loves ya.

CHANDLER. I really need some wine.

LAURA. You don't need wine. You need to come over here.

CHANDLER. I know it's right here! Somewhere!

LAURA. And after wine you'll wanna brush your teeth and floss! Bonzo's gonna think I'm moonlighting.

CHANDLER. What are you doing?

LAURA. Seducing you.

CHANDLER. O.

LAURA. C'mon now, lay your sweet head down on your nice white pillow.

CHANDLER. Pillow! (*He springs up for the pillow, finds the wine under it.*) Eureka! Would you like some?

LAURA. Just a swig.

CHANDLER. Caps so tight.

LAURA. You have to break the metal band first.

CHANDLER. I can't seem to . . .

LAURA. Here.

CHANDLER. Oh, God.

LAURA. You cut?

CHANDLER. On the cap.

LAURA. Oh, shit, you gonna die now?

CHANDLER. My life is not that exciting.

LAURA. Please don't die on me, cupcake.

CHANDLER. I'm fine.

LAURA. Let me call an ambulance.

CHANDLER. No. I'm fine.

LAURA. You faintin'?

CHANDLER. No.

LAURA. Sure?

CHANDLER. Yes.

LAURA. You look pale.

CHANDLER. I'm Caucasian. Thank you.

LAURA. You're so cold.

CHANDLER. I have to rest now.

LAURA. You ain't checkin out, are ya.

CHANDLER. No. Please go!

LAURA. I'll come back some other time.

CHANDLER. Yes. (*CHANDLER gets into bed. LAURA covers him.*)

LAURA. And we can talk about the stars and all.

CHANDLER. Yes.

LAURA. And maybe you'd like to take Walter's Tuesday night slot.

CHANDLER. Please go.

LAURA. Sweetie babe? I need the money.

CHANDLER. But nothing happened.

LAURA. You pay for the time, not the ride, babe.

CHANDLER. I gave it to Scagg.

LAURA. Scagg? He don't take the squirt, boy. I need some paper t' account my time t' Bonzo.

CHANDLER. Scagg's got it.
LAURA. (*grabbing his face*) If you lie, me and Bonzo's coming back. (*Exit LAURA.*)

(*He turns out his light. The sound of a train. CHAND-LER sits up in bed. Sound of a train.*)

CHANDLER. Did you hear about Chandler? He's missing. Not a clue. Left no note. Took nothing. He went forth in the world unemcumbered. Someone saw him among the vagabonds. Someone saw him hitch a freight train.

(*A faint Guazi belly dancer tune as old as the nile, wafts through to him. In it, we must feel the heat of the desert and the mystery of the East. CHANDLER uncovers his head, listens, sits up, listens. The moon appears slowly, so slowly. Subtly indicate a passage of time. CHANDLER goes to his balcony, opens doors, sees the music comes from the light apartment across the alley from his own. He sees the moon.*)

CHANDLER. (*continued*) Cadaverous moon—you pocked-marked thief. —That's not even your own light, but reflected sun. —The only men you ever had left their footprints on you, and never came back. —One side's too cold, one side's too hot. You gloat down with that vicious silence, you swollen lump of a whore's earwax . . .

(*Enter SHIVAREE. She wears the traditional garb of the belly dancer—opaque harem pants, coin bra*

*and girdle, long chiffon veil, tiny bells, bangles,*
*beads, chains, rings, bracelets, earrings and zills on*
*her fingers.*)

SHIVAREE. Sorry if my music woke you. (*She begins*
*to exit.*)
CHANDLER. Excuse me!
SHIVAREE. Yeah?
CHANDLER. It didn't wake me.
SHIVAREE. Goodnight.
CHANDLER. Excuse me.
SHIVAREE. Yeah?
CHANDLER. Sorry if my talking woke you.
SHIVAREE. I wasn't asleep.
CHANDLER. That's — wonderful.
SHIVAREE. Goodnight.
CHANDLER. EXCUSE ME!
SHIVAREE. Yeah?
CHANDLER. Exactly what kind of music is that music
precisely? Greek? Arabic? Israeli?
SHIVAREE. All o'that, and more.
CHANDLER. O?
SHIVAREE. Oriental dance. — (*She begins to exit.*)
CHANDLER. And what's that on your fingers?
SHIVAREE. Zills. (*She demonstrates, but not too*
*much.*)
CHANDLER. I love that sound!
SHIVAREE. (*She sounds them again, very little.*)
Goodnight now.
SHIVAREE. (*After he turns to reenter his room, she*
*reappears.*) My name's Shivaree.
CHANDLER. Shivaree.
SHIVAREE. Ain't m'real name.
CHANDLER. Professional name? I'm Chandler.

SHIVAREE. Wish m'arms was longer.

CHANDLER. Just moved in?

SHIVAREE. Sublet. Passin through.

CHANDLER. The occupants don't usually stay long in those apartments.

SHIVAREE. Well, nice t'meet you.

CHANDLER. Hot.

SHIVAREE. Terrible.

CHANDLER. This night affords a crystalline view of the constellation Hercules.

SHIVAREE. Man alive! Throw an eye at that buttery moon!

CHANDLER. Actually, it's the gibbous phase.

SHIVAREE. Say again?

CHANDLER. More than half but less than full. When it's parameters are convex.

SHIVAREE. You some kind of astronomer?

CHANDLER. That's my bailiwick.

SHIVAREE. You boys still anglin to string that unstrung pearl?

CHANDLER. I beg your pardon.

SHIVAREE. Me, I just let it roll around the night unclaimed.

CHANDLER. You'll love this vantage during thunderstorms, St. Elmo's fire dances on that church steeple.

SHIVAREE. When'd you come south, Yank?

CHANDLER. I was born here.

SHIVAREE. Not talkin' like that.

CHANDLER. I taught myself a provincial dialect now in widespread disuse: Standard American English. Perhaps we could have tea sometime?

SHIVAREE. Sometime's for dreamers. I'm up for it right now.

CHANDLER. Splendid.

SHIVAREE. But not for tea. You got beer?

CHANDLER. No, but I've got some questionable wine.

SHIVAREE. I know the brand well.

CHANDLER. Out front there are two doors. (*She enters her apartment. CHANDLER shouts at her.*) One for the apartments, and my private entrance on the left—just ring the buzzer and . . . (*She reenters with a tubular ironing board and makes a bridge between balconies.*)

CHANDLER. What are you doing?

SHIVAREE. Makin' a bridge, sport. Let down your locks, Rapunzel, I'm a' comin over.

CHANDLER. Not on that!

SHIVAREE. Ain't the Golden Gate, but it gets ya there.

CHANDLER. O my God. (*She jumps onto his balcony.*)

SHIVAREE. Hi. Well, ain't this a kick in the ol' wazoo.

CHANDLER. What is this?

SHIVAREE. Coins.

CHANDLER. I've never seen anyone dress like this!

SHIVAREE. Well, there was a time way way back in Egypt when a man was so scarce that a woman had to wear her coins and do alittle dance in the marketplace t'attract one.—Woolworths.

CHANDLER. And what's your purpose?

SHIVAREE. I'm warmin up for a show t'night.

CHANDLER. O.

SHIVAREE. Private party.

CHANDLER. Won't you sit down? (*A banana falls from the rafters.*) I hang a bunch up in the rafters, and when they're ripe, they fall.

SHIVAREE. Jus' like ol' what's-his-bucket? An apple fell and he invented the law of gravity?

CHANDLER. Newton. Well, actually, he didn't invent

it. He merely described and formulated a law based upon observation.

SHIVAREE. So what are you formulatin' with fallin' bananas?

CHANDLER. It's not an experiment. — They're more nutritious when they're ripe.

SHIVAREE. Why don't you just keep 'em down here and eat 'em when they're ripe?

CHANDLER. You never know for sure. You can't tell just by the outer coloring. When it's truely ripe, a chemical reaction occurs, the stem weakens, and it falls when its ready.

SHIVAREE. Ahhhh.

CHANDLER. Tell me about your profession.

SHIVAREE. You could pluck out m'fingernails and I wouldn't reveal the sacred mysteries of the dance. Disclosure's punishable by artha-ritic hips.

CHANDLER. Why is it sacred?

SHIVAREE. Why, it only celebrates the most important thing in the whole world, that's all, sport.

CHANDLER. Which is?

SHIVAREE. Man and woman.

CHANDLER. O.

SHIVAREE. I saw belly-dancers in the murals on the tombs in Egypt, with zills on their fingers.

CHANDLER. You've been to Egypt?

SHIVAREE. Hell, sport, I danced there, in moonlight before the Temple of Isis.

CHANDLER. Where do you dance now?

SHIVAREE. Wherever the power of woman bring new life is appreciated. Sometimes I just drop in a nursing home, dance for the infirm and the old. They're really the best appreciators.

CHANDLER. Can you make a living doing that?

SHIVAREE. Well, sport, you can dance for dance and
get a flat rate, or you can dance for tips and get what
you get. Like after dancin' at the Hyatt last night, seven
sheiks from Dubai approach me and said they was
throwin' some highbrow shindig up in their suite, would
I grace their company with the dance, salam alekum, the
whole bit, and I says, Hell yeah, and I walks in and it
looks like a sheet sale, all kinds of Mideastern folk jab-
berin' and the musicians go big for some Guazi tune and
I let loose my stuff, I do veil work where I put myself in
this envelope like a little chrysalis in a gossamer cacoon
listenin' to the beat of my heart, and then I break out
with hip shimmies and shoulder rolls and belly flutters,
mad swirls, Byzantine smiles and half-closed eyes, and
my hands are cobras slitherin' on air, hoods open and
I'm Little Egypt, Theodora, Nefertiti, and Salome, all in
one skin, and these before me was Solomon and Herod
and Caeser and Tutankhamen shoutin' Ayawah,
Shivaree, Ayawah, which roughly means, Go for it, little darlin'—and this young sheik he's clappin hands to
my zills, and he rolls up this hundred dollar bill and tries
to slip it in my clothes, which makes me stop dancin',
which makes the musicians stop, and there's this hush
when I fling that hundred dollar bill on the rug, and it
gets so quiet you could hear a rat tiptoe on cotton, and I
says, Look here, sucker, I'm a dancer, and I'm moved by
Ishtar, Aphrodite, Venus, Isis, Astarte, and Rickee Lee
Jones, all them sultry ladies of the East. I am the goddess of the feathery foot, and I only take orders from
the moon. Direct. I have turned dives into temples,
cadavers into footstompers, drunks into believers, and
Tuesday night into Sunday mornin' gospel-time, and I
don't take tips. It ain't proper to tip a goddess. And I
starts to leave in a huff, and the young sheik comes to

'pologize, asks me to Arabia, he would take care o' everything, and then I know he's talkin about the even more ancient horizontal-dance of the harem girl, and I says, Tell me, sheik, you got biscuits 'n gravy over there? And he says, What's biscuits and gravy? And I walks out sayin, See there, sheik, you're living a deprived life, — And that's m'story bub, now where's this wine?

CHANDLER. Wine? — O, yes — of course. But what time's your dancing engagement?

SHIVAREE. Fifteen minutes ago.

CHANDLER. So you have to leave soon?

SHIVAREE. After alittle vino. Let 'em wait. Just a pack o' apes lookin for a thrill. — What's this for, Tommy Peeps? (*He pours wine into soft plastic cups.*)

CHANDLER. I observe the stars.

SHIVAREE. And maybe an occasional lighted window?

CHANDLER. I find the movements in the heavens more interesting.

SHIVAREE. I admire your principles. So, you're a star-man, eh? What's these pictures here?

CHANDLER. Various heavenly phenomena: nebulae and comets, double stars, Jupiter's moons, star clusters, our moon itself. (*She spins planets in a model of the solar system.*)

SHIVAREE. And what's this big swirly pizza-thing?

CHANDLER. That's our galaxy. Our solar system is a little dot about — here.

SHIVAREE. You mean all of those planets is just an itsy-bitsy dot?

CHANDLER. Our solar system is one of billions in this universe.

SHIVAREE. You think there's life out there?

CHANDLER. It's estimated there are 50,000 planets in our galaxy with earthlike conditions.

SHIVAREE. But how'd ya get these pictures?

CHANDLER. I mount a camera on the telescope. It has a self-adjusting device to compensate for the earth's motion. (*handing her wine*) Please don't touch the setting. It's fixed on a star.

SHIVAREE. Can I look-see?

CHANDLER. Do you see a cluster of three stars?

SHIVAREE. Yeah.

CHANDLER. Do you see one of the stars brighter than the others? Kind of pulsating?

SHIVAREE. Yeah!

CHANDLER. That's Eta Carinae, the largest star in our Milky Way.

SHIVAREE. It looks about the same as the others size-wize.

CHANDLER. It's further away. — Nine thousand light years, which is the distance light travels in a vacuum in one sidereal year. — About six million million miles times nine thousand.

SHIVAREE. Eta Carinae.

CHANDLER. It's a blue supergiant, one hundred times bigger than our sun, and will explode, soon.

SHIVAREE. Tonight?

CHANDLER. By cosmological standards, soon is anytime in the next one-hundred thousand years.

SHIVAREE. How come she's explodin'?

CHANDLER. The star is a supernova: it has consumed itself. — Burned itself up from within. — And is about to collapse at which time it will unleash the heat and light of a billion suns.

SHIVAREE. A billion suns! Explodin' stars! Nine thousand light years! You ever come down here with the rest of us?

CHANDLER. I ceased bein an earthling after my first parachute jump.

SHIVAREE. You do that?

CHANDLER. My life was cleaved in two: pre-jump and post jump. You hold on the wingbrace waiting for the jumpmaster to nod. You must believe that nylon, folded in a certain way, can subterfuge gravity. He nods. This is it. Let go. One-one thousand, two-one thousand, three-one thousand, you fall away. The Piper-Cub's just a toy. You leave the heaviness of flesh, become pure spirit, sublime as sunlight shafting through cumulonimbus. Four, five, six one-thousand. The earth nears and reminds you're no more than a gnat whirling. Seven, eight, nine, ten one-thousand. Find the ripcord. Pull. The miracle happens. A fabulous nylon cherry blossom puffs up so pretty overhead and prolongs the ecstasy.

SHIVAREE. Praise the lord.

CHANDLER. You yell like a baby out of womb, and as you drumble towards the earth, you know, this is it, this is really it.

SHIVAREE. Man alive. How do you support all these bad habits?

CHANDLER. I'm a astrobiophycist. (*pause*) I'm in the manufacture of life saving drugs that are made in their purest form in a zero gravity environment.

SHIVAREE. But—can you name the Seven Dwarfs?

CHANDLER. Can you name the constellations?

SHIVAREE. I never saw one.

CHANDLER. I'll show you it's interstellar geometry. It's just connecting the stars with imaginary chalk.

SHIVAREE. You think the maker put each star up there like he was decoratin a wedding cake? or just sorta slung 'em across the sky like popcorn t'pigeons?

CHANDLER. I think he started to fix each one in order, but found chaos more interesting. But we imposed order on the chaos, made pictures with the stars, called them Cassiopeia's Chair, Hercules . . .

SHIVAREE. Now just how do you see a Hercules in all that jumble?

CHANDLER. It's between Corona Borealis and the Lyre.

SHIVAREE. Now make believe you're talkin to a centipede.

CHANDLER. Follow my finger. That's the sky.

SHIVAREE. I'm with ya so far.

CHANDLER. Three stars?

SHIVAREE. I'm goin strong.

CHANDLER. That's Hercules' club.

SHIVAREE. Lost me.

CHANDLER. It's like the meaty part of a turkey leg.

SHIVAREE. Got it.

CHANDLER. Follow the finger to one star.

SHIVAREE. I'm there.

CHANDLER. That's his fist, holding the drumstick.

SHIVAREE. If you say so. Where's the rest of 'em?

CHANDLER. (*on bed*) Alright, this is the sky—imagine Hercules on right knee, club raised, left hand before him, left leg thus,—all upside down.

SHIVAREE. Still don't see it, bub.

CHANDLER. It's difficult to picture the picture instantaneously. Perhaps if you were to lie down on the bed upside down.

SHIVAREE. Hell, you star-gazers are slicker than hogs in slime.

CHANDLER. Your assumption as to my motive is entirely erroneous.

SHIVAREE. I ain't never seen a pair o' pants who didn't

talk true blue who wasn't really thinkin' screw you.

CHANDLER. I regard myself as something more than a pair of pants. —

SHIVAREE. Good night, starman.

CHANDLER. No. Think what you want. But I am not that.

SHIVAREE. I'm so used t'apes maulin me when I dance, I can't tell a bonafide man anymore. (*pause*) I'll take that wine now. (*Pause, he fills both cups.*) I got a sudden case o' the dancer's jimjams.

CHANDLER. What do you mean?

SHIVAREE. That's when you think yourself a temple dancer whirlin through the incense, and look in the spectators' eye and see a cheap strip-tease. — To starting over. (*She offers a toast. They touch cups, drink, cough.*)

CHANDLER. Sorry.

SHIVAREE. You said it was questionable. Question is: will we live?

CHANDLER. Why do you keep dancing for apes?

SHIVAREE. This is what I was born for. If there's one appreciator among the pack, I'll wear m'feet down to the ankle. Once I was dancin in this Sicilian bistro and this dude Lodovico was pealin an orange in one hand, leavin the rind in one piece, unbroke, and I thought, Damn, any man who could be that gentle with an orange, must be something else with a lady, and he starts talkin cotton-candy and out t'sea on his yacht Il Caprice he slips a Spanish fly in m'wine.

CHANDLER. Then what?

SHIVAREE. Strap on your seat-belt, sport. — I let him have the Roman special. — Stuck a finger down m'throat, upchucked all over that orange-pealin wizzbag, leaped in the Mediterranean, swam t'shore.

CHANDLER. What do you do for excitement?

SHIVAREE. O, — I work m'regular job.

CHANDLER. Which is?

SHIVAREE. I read feet.

CHANDLER. Pardon?

SHIVAREE. You heard o' palmistry? Well, this is pedistry. It's more accurate. I see you're from Missouri. Off your shoe and sock, peach fuzz. C'mon, c'mon, I'll read the future.

CHANDLER. That's frivolous.

SHIVAREE. Sure it is, sure it is, — till it comes true.

CHANDLER. You don't really set store by it, do you?

SHIVAREE. Off your shoe and sock, infidel, 'less you're afraid.

CHANDLER. Afraid of what?

SHIVAREE. Why, t'have all your shaky beliefs come crashin' down in a stinkin' junkheap, — that's what. (*He laughs and takes off his shoe and sock.*)

CHANDLER. Predict one thing, anything.

SHIVAREE. Silence. You've got a real long lifeline, but . . .

CHANDLER. But what?

SHIVAREE. It's crossed.

CHANDLER. By what?

SHIVAREE. A very strong pain line.

CHANDLER. What's that mean?

SHIVAREE. It means you're a damn fool. (*She digs her fingernail into his instep.*)

CHANDLER. No! Stop! Please! I'll bruise!

SHIVAREE. Fool, fool, go back t'school. (*A banana falls, scares them both. They laugh. She grabs his hand and pulls him into a kiss.*) Now don't go fallin' in love with me or your name's just gone straight to the bottom of a long list o'broken hearts. Where'd you ever learn to touch a lady with such angora fingers.

CHANDLER. I read alot.

SHIVAREE. How many wet-eye damsels do ya got in your pretty little palm?

CHANDLER. I never had a girlfriend.

SHIVAREE. You're gonna go far in this world, peach fuzz, 'cause you lie with such a God-love-ya smile.

CHANDLER. It's the truth.

SHIVAREE. Kiss me, peach fuzz, afore I yawn t'death. Soon, and I ain't talkin' cosmological soon. (*kiss*) M'grand-daddy can do better than that. I gotta go.

CHANDLER. Don't go.

SHIVAREE. Give me a reason to stay.

CHANDLER. I got reasons. — I got a hundred and forty million reasons!

SHIVAREE. That's enough for me! Let it take all night. Let's go get some proper vino, and I challenge you to barefoot one handed frisbee on the levee — best out o' three — and I'll dance for you, special. C'mon, peach fuzz! Say yes! Move, statue afore your feet take root!

CHANDLER. I can't.

SHIVAREE. C'mon! Let's break rowdy on a midnight binge!

CHANDLER. I can't go outside.

SHIVAREE. Ol Eta's gonna explode and release enough heat and light t'vaporize us! If I get time, I'll compare ya to the moon. C'mon.

CHANDLER. I'm a hemophiliac. A bleeder.

SHIVAREE. C'mon, peach-fuzz, you gotta rise before the rooster t'razzle me!

CHANDLER. I wanted to tell you before, but you made me forget. (*pause*) I rarely go out. Even then, it's in the backseat of a padded cab that my mother drives to support me. And that's to the Emergency room for transfusion, dentist, museum, library, sometimes restaurants. (*pause*) Classic hemophelia. The inability to form a plasma protein, Factor VII. Which makes thrombin. Which converts fibrinogen to fibrin. Which clots blood. Which means you don't run barefoot on the levee. Or jump from airplanes. Or anything else. (*pause*) It's a myth you can die from a scratch. You don't die. You ooze for days. You lay still. You read. You think. Alot. Too much. Of a lifetime of premeditated babysteps across a room. All owing to the minutest biochemical snafu on a strand of mom's DNA. You retreat from the world because you bruise easily. You befriend paranoia. The room's full of assassins. A lightbulb. That table's corner. The door jamb. Anything. That's every moment's dread: Bumping. Bruising. Hemorrhage in joints, degradation of bone and cartilage, or within muscle. Rig the I.V., insert the needle. Lay still. Plastic bag of somebody else's plasma. Alot of cab fares. Thus the padding. (*pause*) This is my domain. You might call me Master of Insignificance. I know every wall crack, every knot in the wood, the bird nests in the treetops, the comings and goings of every neighbor in my field of vision, and the stars.

SHIVAREE. Take off your shoe and sock.

CHANDLER. Why?

SHIVAREE. To see what I did t' your foot.

CHANDLER. It's fine.

SHIVAREE. Take off your shoe and sock.

CHANDLER. No, it's alright.

SHIVAREE. You will or I will. (*She looks at his sole.*) Why didn't you stop me? Why didn't you tell me? Why didn't you make me stop?

CHANDLER. I wanted you to touch me.

(*Enter MARY, with an ice cream bag. An unendurable pause.*)

CHANDLER. It's just a scratch. Of all things, on the air conditioner.

MARY. (*long pause*) Who are you?

CHANDLER. I'd like you to meet —

MARY. Chandler!

SHIVAREE. (*pause*) My name is Shivaree, ma'am.

MARY. Who are you?

SHIVAREE. I'm your new neighbor. — Chandler just took me on a little tour of the cosmos.

MARY. What are you doing here?

SHIVAREE. I live right across the way, ma'am.

MARY. But what are you doing in this house!

SHIVAREE. Me and Chandler, we're friends.

MARY. How long has this been?

SHIVAREE. O, it's hard to say.

CHANDLER. An hour.

MARY. You know Chandler's condition?

CHANDLER. She didn't know, Mom.

MARY. This is a sick boy here — and I work too long and too hard to keep him in blood or to let him keep company with a whore . . .

CHANDLER. Mom —

MARY. You shush!

SHIVAREE. Ma'am, I happen to take huge exception to your fly-off the handle remarks, but it's no sooner said then overlooked. I am a very high-class terpischorean.

MARY. You will never come in this house again.

SHIVAREE. Ma'am?

MARY. Never. Get out.

SHIVAREE. Chandler? (*CHANDLER turns away. Pause. SHIVAREE walks through the French doors onto the balcony.*)

MARY. Where are you going? (*SHIVAREE walks over to the bridge. SHIVAREE pulls the bridge away and exits. MARY closes the doors, closes the window, turns on the air conditioner. Pause. She looks at CHANDLER's wound, gets the first aid kit, puts on a new dressing, not because it's necessary, but because she has always been the one to do this. Long pause.*) Did you sleep with her?

CHANDLER. No.

MARY. I want the truth?

CHANDLER. NO! (*MARY slaps him.*)

MARY. Baby!

## BLACKOUT

## END OF ACT ONE

# ACT TWO

*SHIVAREE's music plays. The next evening. Lights up slowly. CHANDLER in a robe and pajama bottoms sits with his back to the audience. He is connected to his I.V. and languidly twirls an orange in one hand, trying to peel it with one hand. The rind breaks. The peal drops. He stands as though to look at SHIVAREE's apartment. Listening to her music.*

CHANDLER. Did you hear about Chandler? They found him dead. O.D. Vitamin C. (*The buzzer sounds. He ignores it. He answers it, wheeling the I.V. stand with him without disconnecting it. When he turns we see that the side of his face is black and blue.*) Who's there?

LAURA. (*over intercom*) I want m'money, cupcake.

CHANDLER. Get it from Scagg! (*He walks away. The buzzer becomes an elongated blare.*) Go away.

LAURA. Open up or I'll ask your mama for it. (*He releases the doorlock, wheels the stand to his desk, sits, picking up orange peels. Enter LAURA.*) I've been took by slick-ass sharpies, I been took by credit card conventioneers, but I never been took by a mother-lovin' zit-face virgin boy. (*LAURA sees his bruise.*) Did I do that? I only just touched your face.

CHANDLER. It wasn't you.

LAURA. What's all this?

CHANDLER. Plasma.

LAURA. My man Bonzo's said your bread or your head.

CHANDLER. I gave the money to Scagg.

LAURA. I ran into Scagg last night. He says he never saw a dime.

CHANDLER. That son-of-a-bitch.

LAURA. Bonzo's pissed.

44

CHANDLER. Would he take a stereo or radio or something?

LAURA. Bonzo only takes foldin' stuff, kid.

CHANDLER. Can I pay him — in a few months?

LAURA. He's gonna scramble my face.

CHANDLER. I gave all my money to Scagg. Fifteen months of my mother's pocketchange. My ice cream money. Twenty five cents a day. A dollar-seventy-five a week. About seven dollars a month in quarters, dimes, nickels, that I hoarded, sorted, wrapped, counted, hid, re-counted, and planned down to the penny for nothing.

LAURA. You shoulda ate the ice cream, boy.

CHANDLER. I know.

LAURA. But ya can't put the python t'sleep with a fudgie-wudgie, though. (*The buzzer sounds. CHAND-LER goes to it, stops.*)

LAURA. It might be Bonzo. (*buzzer*) He chews doors like this for breakfast.

CHANDLER. How did this happen!

LAURA. Answer it. (*CHANDLER wheels standard to door-release button.*)

CHANDLER. Who's there?

SCAGG. M'man!

CHANDLER. Scagg!

LAURA. Let him up! I want my money!

CHANDLER. (*releasing the door lock*) Why am I such an invertebrate? Ring bell, salivate. I can't say no. I can't say yes. I'm just a knee-jerk.


(*Enter SCAGG in filthy clothes, his right hand wrapped in a bloody rag. CHANDLER stands behind stan-dard.*)

SCAGG. Your ma booted me—garbage-bagged m'threads, put 'em out on the curb, flushed three thou worth o' blow down the john, all cause you went and told her I gave you a magazine. Now the supplier's hatchets shived me in the penny arcade said come up with the paper or the stuff or they're gonna put me t'bed with a shovel tonight. Now I got to skip this dogass town—and don't have no clothes. Gimmie some clothes.

CHANDLER. Where's Laura's money?

SCAGG. This it? (*CHANDLER doesn't move.*)

CHANDLER. You took fifty. She only charges thirty-five.

SCAGG. M'man! I'm bleedin' 'cause o' *you!*

LAURA. Simmer down, you. (*CHANDLER grabs the clothes from SCAGG.*)

CHANDLER. Get out.

SCAGG. I need them threads, bro.

LAURA. Give him the damn clothes, dumbass.

CHANDLER. Get out of here. (*SCAGG retakes the clothes.*)

SCAGG. I could put you away so easy. (*CHANDLER pushes SCAGG.*)

CHANDLER. Pussy.

SCAGG. Do it again and see what happens. (*CHANDLER pushes SCAGG.*)

CHANDLER. Pussy.

SCAGG. You gonna die. (*CHANDLER pushes SCAGG.*)

CHANDLER. C'mon, pussy! Put me away! (*SCAGG grabs CHANDLER by the robe, picks him up. Pause.*)

LAURA. C'mon, the boy ain't right in his brain. (*Pause. SCAGG puts CHANDLER down. CHANDLER spits in SCAGG's face. LAURA stands between. SCAGG pushes her away.*) You got no sense, boy.

CHANDLER. You pussy.

SCAGG. You *wanna* die.

LAURA. Boy, can't you tell your life from a mess o' rags?

CHANDLER. Why don't you put me away, pussy?

SCAGG. (*pause*) 'Cause I'm a nice guy. (*SCAGG counts out some money on the floor. Exit SCAGG. CHANDLER picks it up, hands it to LAURA. Long pause.*)

LAURA. Don't care too much for life, do ya?

CHANDLER. What's a life worth these days?

LAURA. More than this. (*LAURA begins to exit.*)

CHANDLER. So much? — Have a profitable night.

LAURA. I can't give back the money, but I do owe you one.

CHANDLER. Let's call it a transaction without the action.

LAURA. I didn't charge you for the house call.

CHANDLER. Your business ethics are only surpassed by your personal morals.

LAURA. Business is business.

CHANDLER. Tautology is tautology and nonsense is nonsense.

LAURA. I seen so many college boys like you before. They pay me with money daddy set aside for their education, take off clothes and stand naked before life afraid to say, Teach me. In ten minutes I make 'em feel like lusty bulls and off they go. Many a happy female out there owes me thanks.

CHANDLER. Mother Teresa was wrongly rewarded.

LAURA. But for you, I have never failed t'raise the rammer.

CHANDLER. I'm above that.

LAURA. I had 'em all and you ain't no different. You

need a good hard toss in the sack. You need alittle woman love in your life.

CHANDLER. Love. — Just another appendix. — Only time you know it's there's when it's ready to burst and kill you. — Love. What you mean's the pedestrian excuse for the exercise of our reptilian physiology — feelgoodism for Cro-Magnon man and woman modernized in permapress polyester — good for a grunt and a squabble, and ulcer, acouple unwanted offspring, and a divorce lawyer's fee . . . Not for me. — I, look down on the chaotic, futile, stinking antheap — and see the humanbugs building Taj Mahals with orange peels, and I veer off, circumnavigating the scope of human knowledge . . . A universal mind . . . One . . . Hermaphroditic . . . Inscrutable . . . Happy.

LAURA. Underneath all that bookstuff, you're a hot-assed Indian. See that thing there, boy? Looks like a bed, eh? It's more. It's the final exam. If that's good, life's good. If that's dogmeat, nothing else's right. Some things you can't learn between book covers. You can bluff yourself inside out but you never took the final exam. You never had a woman.

CHANDLER. Once.

LAURA. Once upon a time.

CHANDLER. That's right.

LAURA. Who was she?

CHANDLER. A dancer.

LAURA. I was a dancer once.

CHANDLER. She was a real dancer.

LAURA. I worked the Ginger Palace right out o' high school. What style go-go she do?

CHANDLER. Danse orientale. --Egyptian style.

LAURA. Belly dancer?

CHANDLER. Pharaonic.

LAURA. 'Scuse me. — Was it good with her?

CHANDLER. Ineffable.

LAURA. So after the first time, you put the python t'sleep and the whole world can take a flush, eh? (*pause*) She dance for ya?

CHANDLER. Of course.

LAURA. Stir ya?

CHANDLER. To the marrow.

LAURA. How'd you meet?

CHANDLER. I met her one night . . . before the Temple of Isis.

LAURA. Is that that pink bar down on Mohamud Ali Boulevard?

CHANDLER. It's a ruins.

LAURA. O.

CHANDLER. In Egypt.

LAURA. O.

CHANDLER. On the Nile.

LAURA. Why was you there?

CHANDLER. I was digging for artifacts. I had just unearthed a bronze statue, utterly lifelike, of goddess Isis, when I heard zills.

LAURA. What's zills?

CHANDLER. Finger cymbals. She was dancing under the moon playing her zills, barefoot on the weathered stone, hair whirling about . . . zills.

LAURA. What's she like?

CHANDLER. She smiles and you'd think the world were a charm on her bracelet. She laughs, throws her head way back, shuts her eyes like she's kissing herself, and you could almost believe she had a summer cottage on the moonshore of Mare Tranquillitatis. (*LAURA does a poor Pharaonic dance.*)

LAURA. She's dancin Egyptian for ya . . . Pretend it's her.

CHANDLER. That's sick.

LAURA. Everybody does it.

CHANDLER. Stop — stop — stop.

LAURA. What's the matter with you?

CHANDLER. The matter is me that I am matter, and matter, having extension in time and space, exerting gravitational attraction to other such bodies, and having *inertia,* resistance to acceleration, quantitatively measured by mass which in this case seems to predominate over the impulse to say . . . I want her.

LAURA. Someday girl you're gonna need a degree for this work.

CHANDLER. Shivaree!

LAURA. You are fargone.

CHANDLER. If there were world enough and time, I would sweeten the air with eloquence, but for now, accept this — Scram.

LAURA. You win, kid.

CHANDLER. Shivaree!

LAURA. Don't chew no razor blades. (*Exit LAURA.*)

CHANDLER. *I am astronomical!* (*Silence. He rushes to his desk, gets a metal cup, dumps the pencil, seizes the metal garbage can, empties it on the floor, rushes to the balcony and makes a shivaree banging them together.*) Hey, hootchy kootch! Get out here, you juicy little enchalada!

(*Enter SHIVAREE in a plain dress.*)

SHIVAREE. What'd you call me?

CHANDLER. I wish I had a bouquet of dirty socks to throw across.

SHIVAREE. What kind o' vino's talkin to me tonight?

CHANDLER. But let this suffice, my apogee, my perigee, my jalapena, my decaffeinated canary! (*He grabs a half dozen multi-colored socks from his dresser and throws them at her.*)

SHIVAREE. (*catching the bouquet*) And they said romance is dead.

CHANDLER. Shivaree, come back and play your zills? There's nothing in this world more beautiful than you playing your zills.

SHIVAREE. I can't never resist a real live appreciator. I'll get 'em. (*She exits. He unplugs the c.b. She reenters with zills and a shoebox tied up with a hair ribbon. She makes her bridge and crosses.*) Where's your ma?

CHANDLER. Gone.

SHIVAREE. So how's your chromosomes, sport? (*She sees his discolored face. She touches it.*)

CHANDLER. I bumped a door in the dark.

SHIVAREE. You keep practicin that, bub, and maybe you'll fool a fool. I got you a little goin away present.

CHANDLER. Where are you going?

SHIVAREE. (*picking up an orange peel, eating an orange slice*) Not bad for a first-timer.

CHANDLER. You can't be unpacked yet.

SHIVAREE. Open it. — I was gonna get you a madras jacket, but hell, if you get caught in the rain, it could bleed t'death. (*He opens the box, takes out a rose.*) I took the thorns off. (*He takes out other things.*) Bull's ears. Dedicated to me by El Matador Juanito at Guadalajara in which he was severely gored in the left cheek o' his butt. That's a tape of them Guazi tunes you like. Camel-bone ring from Kabul which wards off desert jinnis, and brings good luck on caravans and dangerous crossings. It's more of a treasure than a present, ain't it? — And there's a big fat bag o blood waiting for ya down at the clinic.

CHANDLER. You gave blood?

SHIVAREE. What's the proper thing t'say to a hemophiliac on such a grand occasion? — Coagulations. What's it called when they take blood, spin off the plasma, and put the red cells back in ya?

CHANDLER. Plasmaphresis.

SHIVAREE. I was the first one in line. Told 'em put it in your account. They all knew who ya were. Everybody say hi.

CHANDLER. Did it hurt?

SHIVAREE. Them suckers rammed me with a needle big as a telephone pole. But it hurts kind of beautiful when you see your blood coursin' through the clear plastic tubes, how red and rich, how quick it fattens the bag with life, and gives ya a Sunday-mornin after-church kind of feelin when the nurse takes her thick black pen and prints like a first-grader on the bag — CHANDLER KIMBROUGH. Knocks the bejesus outta me to think our plasmas are gonna mix in your veins. — So when you get a transfusion and start shakin those hips and talkin twang, don't wonder why.

CHANDLER. Where will you go?

SHIVAREE. Memphis.

CHANDLER. What's there?

SHIVAREE. Home.

CHANDLER. For how long?

SHIVAREE. Till m'vocal cords're stripped from screamin-match with my folks. They don't approve o' no female over twenty who don't have three wailin brats hangin on her leg.

CHANDLER. After that?

SHIVAREE. I'm liable t'chase the first dandylion fuzz-ball t'come along.

CHANDLER. And then come back.

SHIVAREE. What for?

CHANDLER. *What for?*

SHIVAREE. That's American for porqué.

CHANDLER. It was my distinct impression . . . I thought we had something between us.

SHIVAREE. We do. Your mama.

CHANDLER. I never had this problem before.

SHIVAREE. I'm sorry I'm gummin' up the works here.

CHANDLER. I don't mean problem. It's always been just mom and me. Who I am and who she is — sometimes blurs.

SHIVAREE. When you sit on a tack, who says ouch, you or her?

CHANDLER. I do.

SHIVAREE. Take thought, bub.

CHANDLER. I can't exist in the world on my own. I was born incomplete. I'm attached to a needle, to a tube, to a plasma bag, to her . . .

SHIVAREE. Save it for your diary. You're as free as you want to be.

CHANDLER. So you're leaving?

SHIVAREE. I already broke the lease.

CHANDLER. Perhaps you can reinstate it.

SHIVAREE. New tenant's moving in tomorrow noon.

CHANDLER. You won't come back?

SHIVAREE. I'll fall back here like a Newton banana if I feel some kind of gravity.

CHANDLER. You never danced for me.

SHIVAREE. I was about to — when you come down with a sudden case o' hemophilia.

CHANDLER. Well—you said you would—so—dance.

SHIVAREE. There's a proper way t'ask, and that ain't it.

CHANDLER. I remind you, I have the disease of kings, and kings don't ask.

SHIVAREE. I remind you, I ain't no dancin concubine on her toes when the king makes a snappy finger, bub.

CHANDLER. I humbly solicit your pardon.

SHIVAREE. I'll think upon it.

CHANDLER. That would please us immeasurably.

SHIVAREE. I'll dance for an unbroken orange peel.

CHANDLER. It's impossible.

SHIVAREE. Lodovico did it.

CHANDLER. No, no. I can't do it. Therefore he can't. I'm ambidextrous and went through three sacks already. Can't be done.

SHIVAREE. Takes a lifetime.

CHANDLER. The slightest twitch and the rind breaks.

SHIVAREE. If devotion was easy, it'd be a rusty beer-can in the gutter.

CHANDLER. Where do you find devotion in a monkey trick?

SHIVAREE. It shows a man willin t'take his sweet time t'denude the fruit.

CHANDLER. It shows a decadent overweening egocentric world-class flim-flam.

SHIVAREE. For all his failings, Lodovico had hands that could teach tenderness to swansdown.

CHANDLER. So tender you jumped ship and swam for your life!

SHIVAREE. Don't get all shook just cause you can't cut the finesse.

CHANDLER. Spare me your fond reminiscences of failed romances. And keep you bulls' ears and your

matador lovers. I don't have hundred dollar bills to
slip in your clothes and I can't unpeal an orange one-
handedly, but for a dance, my eyes will pay tribute.
    SHIVAREE. Tribute I will take. Put on that tape, sport.
(*She lights votive candles.*) Lie down. There's an ancient healing dance called the Zar. It drives out demons
called afreetees, like the one you got in your
chromosome. (*The music begins.*)
    CHANDLER. Why?
    SHIVAREE. No talk. Lie down.
    CHANDLER. Where'd you learn this?
    SHIVAREE. In Istanbul. From an old leper woman
with a milky white eye. She sent me t'study the Naja-
Naja cobra up there in Punjabi. When some intrudin
animal goes near her nest, she stands, puffs her hood,
and bobs and weaves and shimmies and sways so pretty,
the intruder gets hypnotized and she bites! — And it's
beddie-bye for eternity. When I stop, life comes up
roses or rhubarb. If this don't grab your butt, you ain't
got one. (*She dances to music that mimics the cobra, us-
ing a makeshift veil. The belly dance becomes the Zar,
the healing dance. She goes to her knees and invites him
into the dance, which he joins shyly. They join hands
and the healing dance becomes the mating dance.*)
    CHANDLER. All my life I've been lovesick without a
lover, till now.
    SHIVAREE. All my life I never found that hand that
could turn me into eiderdown, till now.
    CHANDLER. I was all secret desire.
    SHIVAREE. I was all tinder and never found fire.
    CHANDLER. You are codeine, morphine, percadan
and demerol.
    SHIVAREE. Hell, I ain't never been compared to a
drugstore before.

CHANDLER. Will you come back?

SHIVAREE. Don't the swallows always fly back to Capistrano?

CHANDLER. Don't go.

SHIVAREE. Beg and bribe me. I'm corrupt like that.

CHANDLER. I'm free-falling and afraid to pull the rip-cord. (*She gently lifts him to his feet and leads him to the bed.*)

SHIVAREE. One one thousand.

CHANDLER. Two one thousand. (*She begins to undress him, only played in silhouette.*)

SHIVAREE. Three one thousand.

CHANDLER. Four one thousand. (*He begins to undress her.*)

SHIVAREE. Five one thousand.

CHANDLER. Six one thousand.

SHIVAREE. Seven one thousand.

CHANDLER. Eight one thousand.

SHIVAREE. Nine one thousand. (*They're in bed under the covers.*) Say it.

CHANDLER. Ten one thousand. (*pause*) Look at us!

SHIVAREE. Ain't we something? What's all this?

CHANDLER. Scars from needles.

SHIVAREE. See here? When I was seven, a big ugly purple grackle flew into me. That's where the beak stuck. And this one's from when I was eleven and Bobby Ray tried to kiss me and I said no and he tried to stick a bumble bee in m'ear and I kicked him and he sicked his dog on me and I bit his dog's ear off. (*They look up through the open skylight.*)

CHANDLER. Do you think there's life out there?

SHIVAREE. I think two red-eye Jupiterians are looking down here right now and one's sayin, You think there's life on that greenish-bluish foggy little ball down there?

CHANDLER. And what's the other one say?

SHIVAREE. She says, Aww, fuzzbrain, what's freckles matter on a shaggy dog? Quit your yip-yap and come lay a juicy liplock on your lovin' lady.

CHANDLER. And then what?

SHIVAREE. And he does so.

CHANDLER. If my heart were put on a scale now, it would balance with a feather. (*SHIVAREE takes one of the votive candles, blows it out, takes the other, holds it before CHANDLER, who blows it out, they recline. They hear footfalls up the stairs. They freeze. Enter MARY.*)

MARY. Lovy?

CHANDLER. Mom!

MARY. Don't get up. Here's Jerry's parachute. But don't get no ideas, sonny boy. You ain't never jumpin'. It's only for that canopy you wanted over the bed. But if it collects dust, out it goes. All day, all damn day, drivin' around with my "Occupied" sign lit up, people lookin' in the empty cab, dispatcher callin', where are ya 409?

CHANDLER. Mom?

MARY. I wasn't strikin' you, lovy. I was strikin' my own face.

CHANDLER. Mom, excuse me . . .

MARY. You got your manly urges I suppose. But God knows this world don't need another bleeder.

CHANDLER. Mom? I'm not alone.

MARY. What?

CHANDLER. Shivaree's here. (*Long pause. MARY turns on the swivel light, aims it at the bed. Long pause.*)

MARY. Get your clothes on.

SHIVAREE. M'am, I strongly object to this.

MARY. You object! Object! You! Get dressed and get out!

SHIVAREE. Would you please turn that light off, m'am?

MARY. O! You got sudden modesty!

CHANDLER. Mom, please. It's difficult enough.

MARY. You! You get out of that filthy bed right now, young man.

CHANDLER. I can't stand up right now.

MARY. No baby steps for you! When you go to hell, you leap headlong in the pit, don't ya? (*MARY turns off the light. CHANDLER and SHIVAREE get out of bed and dress.*)

SHIVAREE. M'am, I'm sorry you caught us in all our dishabille.

MARY. Shameless. Like dogs pairin' up on the lawn at noon. With all your learnin, all your knowledge, you fall for the first one-night flirt that comes along.

CHANDLER. Mom, Shivaree gave blood today, and put it in my name.

MARY. Anybody can give blood. I know vagabonds who give blood 'cause they want that eleven dollars and fifty.

SHIVAREE. I really do care for Chandler, m'am.

MARY. For how many hours? You care for him in leg braces? Wheelchair? You'd curdle at the first sight of blood.

SHIVAREE. I do, m'am.

MARY. How much?

SHIVAREE. M'am?

MARY. How much do ya care?

SHIVAREE. I don't rightly know howt' answer that, m'am. As far as I know, ain't no measure for affections.

MARY. Yessir! Yessir, there's a measure! How still can ya sit when incompetent interns are learnin' their trade on your little baby, when he cuts his tongue on a lollipop and bleeds for a week and they're diggin in his veins t'run a transfusion, diggin and searchin' and probin' in your baby's arm — diggin' — ? O god. Can ya watch a good man take to bottle and put himself in the ground? Can ya be your baby's skin in a world that's a booby trap for him? How much will ya care when the blood don't stop no matter how much gauze and bandages you throw at it, cause the blood wants out! — His blood and my blood, too! I give blood till they won't let me give no more! Can ya force your unwillin lips back over your teeth t'make a smile t'get a tip? How much do you care, little dancin girl?

SHIVAREE. Enough never t'slap his face, m'am.

MARY. You get gone.

CHANDLER. No, stay, please.

SHIVAREE. Bye, star-gazer. You should be sportin Corona Borealis for a diadem, sittin up there in Cassiopeia's Chair, 'cause your gentle ways makes you the natural-born aristocracy o' men. Hail, peach-fuzz. (*Exit SHIVAREE, withdrawing her bridge. MARY rips the sheets off the bed.*)

MARY. In a night you tumble back nineteen years and animalize. Where was your mind? Answer me. Answer. I will be answered.

CHANDLER. You can't talk to me like that anymore.

MARY. I assumed before tonight that you tucked all this away and came to realize . . . you can't be with a woman.

CHANDLER. Like you realized when they said your sons would be bleeders?

MARY. I thought the world would make an exception

in my case.—There's not a second of my life I don't regret it.

CHANDLER. Regret me? Too late. I'm here. And this cubic space can't hold me anymore.

MARY. I only want you to have a good long life.

CHANDLER. Good? What's that mean? Sterile? Then it was superlative. Long? I have been sustained for centuries and never lived until tonight.

MARY. You don't have the injuries of other hemophiliacs.

CHANDLER. I'd rather be Jerry Vollens thrashing in barbed wire dying by spurts and gushes! At least once he lived!

MARY. He could've lived longer!

CHANDLER. For what? Live longer for what?—To stuff a coffin?

MARY. Alls I know is this thing, this godawful thing's got to end with us—

CHANDLER. You mean me, end with me!

MARY. You want to watch your grandsons piercin' veins with the hypo? like you did? eh? and when you didn't cry, I did! while that big strong weakling of a father drank it away with sour mash! Chandler, you have an obligation to the unborn.

CHANDLER. The same obligation you couldn't keep?

MARY. I didn't have your high mind.

CHANDLER. I don't have my highmind either . . . Sometimes I want to kill myself . . . but I don't want to be dead . . . For whatever screwup in a chromosome, I am a man . . . and I want her, mom.

MARY. You're my only family. I live for you. You don't know what I do out there. You don't see me fightin' cabbies for a place in the airport line—you don't see me over-chargin out-o'-towners for you! (*SHIVAREE'S music wafts across the balconies. Pause.*)

CHANDLER. You don't have to punish yourself with work for me. You don't have to do penance for bringing me in the world—because I love you for giving me life,—Look at those stars! burning themselves out!—Me too.—Hell, me too.—I want to hear those zills,—listen, one hundred and forty million sweet Egyptian zills.

MARY. I never knew you had so much vinegar in you, Mr. Kimbrough.

CHANDLER. I never knew pigheadedness is genetically transmitted.

MARY. I am not pigheaded. I am simply addicted to my beliefs.

CHANDLER. We're taking off tomorrow.

MARY. Off?

CHANDLER. The whole day.

MARY. How can I take off?

CHANDLER. You don't show up, and if the world folds up, to hell with 'em. We're going to the races.

MARY. I have a living to make, honeybabe.

CHANDLER. We have to live, too.

MARY. Let's do.

CHANDLER. In the grandstand.

MARY. Alright.

CHANDLER. And then a picnic.

MARY. Chicken and lemonade.

CHANDLER. Enough for three.

MARY. Son of a bee.—Well, Mr. Kimbrough, I'm missin some good business at the airport.

CHANDLER. Why don't you get some sleep?

MARY. No. I wanna drive. I never know what I'm thinkin' till I'm driving. (*pause*) Looks like we're not gettin no sleep round here what with her playing that hootchy kootchy music all night long.

CHANDLER. It's oriental.

MARY. O yeah? What's her name?

CHANDLER. Shivaree. (*MARY nods and exits. CHANDLER listens to her footfalls die away, listens to the door close. He goes out on the balcony, and softly calls.*) Shivaree? (*He reenters, rushes to a bookshelf, topples books onto the floor, makes a bridge between the balconies, stands on the ledge, puts one foot on the bridge, then another foot, looks down, steps back to the ledge, hears the zills tease. The bats flit. The cats caterwaul. The stars burn as they always have. He rushes back into the room, takes the bedspread, makes an Arabian garb for himself, tying SHIVAREE's ribbon about his head. He begins to rush out again, puts on the parachute, stops again, picks up an orange, tosses it in the air, catches it. He rushes to the balcony, takes in the music, surrenders to it, and begins to make his dangerous crossing, slowly, surely, never looking down, balancing carefully his babysteps in the dark. The lights fade quickly as he surmounts the balcony and enters into SHIVAREE's door.*)

THE END

# SKIN DEEP
## Jon Lonoff

*Comedy / 2m, 2f / Interior Unit Set*

In *Skin Deep*, a large, lovable, lonely-heart, named Maureen Mulligan, gives romance one last shot on a blind-date with sweet awkward Joseph Spinelli; she's learned to pepper her speech with jokes to hide insecurities about her weight and appearance, while he's almost dangerously forthright, saying everything that comes to his mind. They both know they're perfect for each other, and in time they come to admit it.

They were set up on the date by Maureen's sister Sheila and her husband Squire, who are having problems of their own: Sheila undergoes a non-stop series of cosmetic surgeries to hang onto the attractive and much-desired Squire, who may or may not have long ago held designs on Maureen, who introduced him to Sheila. With Maureen particularly vulnerable to both hurting and being hurt, the time is ripe for all these unspoken issues to bubble to the surface.

"Warm-hearted comedy ... the laughter was literally show-stopping. A winning play, with enough good-humored laughs and sentiment to keep you smiling from beginning to end."
- TalkinBroadway.com

"It's a little Paddy Chayefsky, a lot Neil Simon and a quick-witted, intelligent voyage into the not-so-tranquil seas of middle-aged love and dating. The dialogue is crackling and hilarious; the plot simple but well-turned; the characters endearing and quirky; and lurking beneath the merriment is so much heartache that you'll stand up and cheer when the unlikely couple makes it to the inevitable final clinch."
- NYTheatreWorld.Com

# WHITE BUFFALO
Don Zolidis

*Drama / 3m, 2f (plus chorus)/ Unit Set*

Based on actual events, WHITE BUFFALO tells the story of the miracle birth of a white buffalo calf on a small farm in southern Wisconsin. When Carol Gelling discovers that one of the buffalo on her farm is born white in color, she thinks nothing more of it than a curiosity. Soon, however, she learns that this is the fulfillment of an ancient prophecy believed by the Sioux to bring peace on earth and unity to all mankind. Her little farm is quickly overwhelmed with religious pilgrims, bringing her into contact with a culture and faith that is wholly unfamiliar to her. When a mysterious businessman offers to buy the calf for two million dollars, Carol is thrown into doubt about whether to profit from the religious beliefs of others or to keep true to a spirituality she knows nothing about.

## COCKEYED
William Missouri Downs

*Comedy / 3m, 1f / Unit Set*

Phil, an average nice guy, is madly in love with the beautiful Sophia. The only problem is that she's unaware of his existence. He tries to introduce himself but she looks right through him. When Phil discovers Sophia has a glass eye, he thinks that might be the problem, but soon realizes that she really can't see him. Perhaps he is caught in a philosophical hyperspace or dualistic reality or perhaps beautiful women are just unaware of nice guys. Armed only with a B.A. in philosophy, Phil sets out to prove his existence and win Sophia's heart. This fast moving farce is the winner of the HotCity Theatre's GreenHouse New Play Festival. The St. Louis Post-Dispatch called Cockeyed a clever romantic comedy, Talkin' Broadway called it "hilarious," while Playback Magazine said that it was "fresh and invigorating."

### Winner!
### of the HotCity Theatre GreenHouse New Play Festival

"Rocking with laughter...hilarious...polished and engaging work draws heavily on the age-old conventions of farce: improbable situations, exaggerated characters, amazing coincidences, absurd misunderstandings, people hiding in closets and barely missing each other as they run in and out of doors...full of comic momentum as Cockeyed hurtles toward its conclusion."
- Talkin' Broadway

CPSIA information can be obtained at www.ICGtesting.com
Printed in the USA
LVOW010618120413

328838LV00002B/48/P

9 780573 619571